Scan the QR code
to read and listen to the
glossary words for FREE!

glossary - *Meanings of words.*

Dados Internacionais de Catalogação na Publicação (CIP) de acordo com ISBD

B964s Burnett, Frances Hodgson
The secret garden - Easier Classics Reading / Frances Hodgson Burnett. – Jandira : W. Books, 2025.
128 p. ; 12,8cm x 19,8cm. – (Easier Classics Reading Library Children's Collection)

ISBN: 978-65-5294-233-3

1. Literatura infantojuvenil. 2. Literatura Infantil. 3. Clássicos. 4. Aventura. 5. Imaginação. 6. Fantasia. I. Título. II. Série.

2025-608

CDD 028.5
CDU 82-93

Elaborado por Vagner Rodolfo da Silva - CRB-8/9410
Índice para catálogo sistemático:
1. Literatura infantojuvenil 028.5
2. Literatura infantojuvenil 82-93

Easier Classics
The Secret Garden

Original story by Frances Hodgson Burnett.
Text based on the adaptation by Gemma Barder.
Illustrations by Rebecca Price.

1st edition in 2025
www.cirandacultural.com.br

The Secret Garden

Frances Hodgson Burnett

W. Books

Meet the Characters

Mary Lennox

Martha

Dickon

Colin

Mr Craven

Mrs Medlock

Ben Weatherstaff

Chapter 1

Mary Lennox was ten years old. She lived in a big house in India with her parents.

But she had no friends and her parents never spent any time with her.

Mary only spent time with the **servants**. But she didn't know how to be friends with them. Instead, she only gave them orders.

servants - *People who are paid to do housework, and look after a family and their guests.*

One morning, Mary woke up alone. There were no servants to give her breakfast in bed or to help her get dressed.

Still wearing only her **nightdress**, Mary looked all over the house. But she didn't find anyone.

Mary didn't talk to many people. But today, the house was so quiet it made her feel worried.

nightdress - *A dress that is worn as pyjamas.*

Mary heard voices coming from her parents' bedroom. She listened by the door.

'**Cholera** has made everyone ill,' said a voice she didn't know.

Mary knew that **cholera** could make people very ill. She felt scared, so she ran back to her room and got into bed. Then, she pulled the sheets up to her neck and waited.

Cholera - *A very serious and dangerous illness.*

After many hours, Mary was hungry. But she didn't know how to make food or how to find the kitchen. So, she went to the garden. The garden always made her happy.

Suddenly, she saw a man in a uniform.

'Who are you and why are you here?' he shouted.

Suddenly - *Quickly and not expected to happen.*

Chapter 2

The man in the garden was an army **officer**. He told Mary that her parents had died from cholera.

The army **officer** thought Mary would cry. But she didn't. Mary wasn't very sad because she hadn't known her parents very well.

The army **officer** told Mary she would be going to live with her uncle in England.

officer - *Someone who is in charge of other people in the army.*

Mary's trip from India to England was very long. She sailed across the sea and went on three different trains.

On the way, she had to carry lots of important papers.

These had to be checked by

important people who made sure

she was going the right way.

After this very long trip,

Mary finally arrived in England.

When Mary got off the train, a tall woman walked towards her.

'Are you Mary Lennox?' asked the woman.

Mary nodded and the woman asked Mary to come with her.

The woman's name was Mrs Medlock and she was the **housekeeper** in Mary's uncle's house. The house was called Misselthwaite **Manor**.

housekeeper - Someone that helps to look after and clean a house.

Manor - A big house in the countryside. Often rich people live there.

Mrs Medlock quickly walked up to a **carriage**.

'Get in quickly, we don't have all day,' Mrs Medlock said **sternly**.

Mary got inside and looked out of the window. England was very different to India. England was cold and had lots of green fields.

carriage - An old-fashioned vehicle, usually for a small number of people, which is pulled by horses.

sternly - When someone says something very seriously.

Chapter 3

Mary had never met her uncle. She had not known that she had an uncle or that he lived in England.

'There are many rules in Misselthwaite Manor,' said Mrs Medlock. 'But the most important rule is that you must never disturb Mr Craven.'

'Who's Mr Craven?' Mary asked.

'Mr Craven is your uncle!' said Mrs Medlock. 'But leave him alone. He is still upset about his wife's death.'

Before Mary could ask anything else, she was **distracted** by the green hills of the Missel **Moor** outside her window.

'Sit still,' said Mrs Medlock. 'We're nearly at the manor.'

distracted - When someone cannot think or complete a task because their attention is on something else.

Moor - A hilly area in the countryside, usually covered in grass and a plant called heather.

Misselthwaite Manor was a large stone house.

Mary was met by a **butler** at the big wooden door.

'Mr Craven is busy. The young **miss** must go straight to her room,' said the **butler**.

butler - The main servant of a house. They complete tasks for the owner of the house.

miss - A name for a young girl or a woman who is not married.

They walked up a huge wooden staircase and down a corridor.

As they walked, Mary saw pictures all along the wall. She saw a picture of a young woman who looked just like her!

'That's your mother,' said Mrs Medlock.

Mary felt sad. She realised she had not really known her mother at all.

Chapter 4

The next morning, Mary woke up in her new room. A young **maid** came in to give her breakfast. The **maid**'s name was Martha.

'Shouldn't I get dressed first?' asked Mary.

'If you want to,' replied the **maid**. 'Mr Craven got these dresses for you, so I hope they fit.'

maid - A girl or a woman who is paid to do housework like cleaning, tidying and cooking.

'Dress me in that one,' said Mary, pointing to a green dress.

'Haven't you ever dressed yourself before?' asked the maid.

Mary was confused. The servants in India always helped her get dressed in the morning.

Mary was **embarrassed**, but Martha helped her get dressed.

embarrassed - Feeling uncomfortable or shy about something that has happened.

Mary thought Martha would stay to play with her, but Martha had to get back to work.

So, Mary explored the big house. Then, she walked outside until she found a garden.

The garden had brick walls around the outside and was full of flowers, plants and vegetables.

A small bird with a red chest flew over to Mary.

'That's just Mr Robin, miss!' said a rough voice.

Chapter 5

The rough voice was Ben Weatherstaff. He had been the gardener at Misselthwaite Manor for a very long time.

'I've never seen a robin before. There weren't any in India,' said Mary.

'There's probably quite a lot of things here that you haven't seen before,' said Ben.

'And don't worry about Mr Robin,' said Ben. 'He comes here every year.'

Mary wanted to know all about the garden.

Ben was very kind. He taught her which plants were vegetables and which were **weeds**.

Mary even helped him pull up the **weeds**.

weeds - A plant that grows where it isn't supposed to.

Soon, Mary's hands were covered in dirt and **soil**. But Mary didn't mind. She liked the smell of the **soil**.

The clock **chimed** 12 o'clock. Ben told Mary to go back to the manor for her lunch.

'Thank you, Ben,' said Mary.
'This was fun.'

soil - *Dirt or mud that is used to grow plants.*

chimed - *A ringing noise that is often made by bells.*

When Mary got back to the manor, Mrs Medlock was angry.

'Why is there mud all over you?' Mrs Medlock asked.

Mary was about to reply when she heard someone start crying.

'Go to your room,' Mrs Medlock ordered before she rushed away towards the sound.

Chapter 6

Two weeks passed since Mary had arrived at Misselthwaite Manor. She had not seen her uncle, but she was still enjoying her time at the house.

When Ben was working in the garden, she followed him and asked him questions.

On other days, Mary would walk across Missel Moor.

One day, it began to rain. Mary had to stay in her room until it stopped.

'Have you found the secret garden yet?' asked Martha. 'My mum says Mr Craven's wife loved flowers and built a beautiful garden. But when she died, Mr Craven locked the door and threw away the key!'

Mary really wanted to know more about the secret garden. But she also wanted to learn about Martha's mother.

'What's your mother like?' asked Mary. 'I never really spoke to mine. I don't think she liked me very much. Grown-ups never do.'

Suddenly, Martha ran to Mary and hugged her. Mary had never been hugged before. She didn't know what to do.

'That's not your fault,' said Martha. 'Real families love each other.'

Then Martha told Mary about her family, mainly her brother, Dickon. Mary wished she had a family like Martha's.

Chapter 7

The next day, the rain stopped.

Mary had been dreaming all night about the secret garden. She wanted to find the secret garden and the key to get inside it.

That morning, Mary ran through the house and out past the garden. She waved to Ben as she ran past him.

Mary ran so quickly that she didn't see Martha and bumped into her.

'Sorry, Martha!' said Mary.

'That's okay!' said Martha. 'I told my mum about you, Mary, and she wanted you to have this.'

It was a skipping rope with red wooden handles. Mary held it as if it was **precious**.

precious - *Something that is loved or important.*

Mary forgot all about looking for the secret garden. She wanted to learn to skip. At first it was hard, but then she slowly began to get better.

As she was skipping, the rope got caught on some **ivy**. Mary pulled it away and it **revealed** an old wooden door.

Mary had found it! She had found the door to the secret garden!

ivy - *A green plant that grows on the outside of walls.*

revealed - *Showing or saying something that wasn't known before.*

Mary tried to turn the **rusted** black doorknob. But the door wouldn't open.

She needed a key.

Mr Robin flew down next to a pile of leaves. As Mary looked at Mr Robin, she noticed there was something silver poking out of the top of the leaves. It was the key!

rusted - An orange, reddish covering that forms over old metal.

Mary picked up the key and put it into the lock. *Click.* The door opened!

She stepped inside and saw a messy but beautiful garden.

There were rosebushes and flowers all over the garden. In the middle of the garden was a fountain.

Around the fountain were paths leading to different places in the garden.

Mary walked down one path that led to a white, metal swing.

Although it was rusted, Mary brushed off the dirt and happily sat down on it.

Soon, Mary saw the plants that Ben had told her were weeds.

She began to pull out all the weeds until she had **weeded** a whole **flowerbed**.

Mary found an old wheelbarrow near the garden wall and used it to collect all the weeds.

weeded - To get rid of weeds.

flowerbed - A place where flowers grow.

That evening, Mary told Martha about the secret garden.

Martha was happy, but told Mary to keep it a secret so that the garden didn't get locked away again.

'I'll keep it safe,' said Mary.
'Could your brother help me to tidy the garden?'

Martha smiled and said, 'I'll ask him.'

Chapter 8

The next day, Dickon met Mary at the secret garden.

He gave Mary a bag which had a small spade, a **gardening fork** and thick gloves inside.

'My sister says your hands are always dirty from gardening, so I thought these would help,' he said.

gardening fork - A tool used to move around dirt and mud to get them ready to grow flowers.

Mary wanted to make sure the garden was kept secret. She made Dickon promise not to tell anyone about the garden before they went inside.

Then, Mary pulled the key to the secret garden out of her pocket. She unlocked the door and they went inside.

Together, they worked to tidy the garden as much as they could.

Every day, Mary went to the garden. Sometimes Dickon helped her, but when he didn't, she was still happier than she had ever been in India.

One morning, she didn't go to the garden because she woke up to the sound of someone crying.

It was the same crying she had heard in the corridor days before.

When Martha came in to open the curtains, Mary asked her who was crying.

Martha didn't want to talk about it and started to talk about something else.

'Mr Craven has come home and he wants to see you today. You'd better get ready,' she said, leaving Mary's bedroom.

Later, Mary made her way to her uncle's office and knocked on the door.

'Come in, Mary,' said her uncle.

Her uncle was tall and thin. He looked like Mary's mother, but his hair was much darker.

'Martha's mother said that I have not been treating you well,' said Mr Craven. 'What can I do to make living here better?'

All Mary wanted was a family. But instead, she told Mr Craven that she liked gardening.

'My wife liked gardening,' said Mr Craven. 'I'll ask Ben to get you a **patch**.'

patch - A small area of land where plants and vegetables are grown.

Chapter 9

One day, there was another storm over Missel Moor.

Everyone had to wait inside until it was over.

Mary usually stayed in her room when it rained, but she heard crying again. So, Mary checked that Martha and Mrs Medlock weren't looking and followed the sound of the crying.

After looking all over the house, Mary found the room where the crying was coming from.

She knocked on the door and heard a child's voice answer.

Mary was so shocked to hear another child that she walked straight into the room.

Inside the room, there was a boy lying on a bed.

'How dare you enter my room without **permission**!' said the boy.

Mary told the boy who she was and that her uncle owned the house.

The boy said his name was Colin Craven and his father was Mr Craven.

permission - To let someone do something.

Mary and Colin were cousins.
They were family!

'Why are you always crying?'
asked Mary.

Colin told Mary that he was very sick and couldn't leave his room. Mary said she would come to visit him and play with him every day because family should stay together.

Chapter 10

The next day, the storm had gone, but it was still raining.

Again, Mary waited until Martha and Mrs Medlock were far away. Then, she ran to Colin's room.

Mary jumped into the room and quickly opened the curtains. Colin smiled.

They played together all morning until there was a knock on the door.

Mrs Medlock came in carrying a tray of soup.

'Mary! What are you doing here?' said Mrs Medlock. 'Get out at once! **Master** Craven must not be disturbed!'

Master - A polite name to call a son of an important man. This name is not used anymore.

Mary was about to leave, but Colin stopped her.

'I want Mary to stay. She is my cousin, and when she's here I don't feel ill,' said Colin.

Mrs Medlock didn't know what to say. She **glared** at Mary.

glared - To look at someone in an angry way.

Colin was Mr Craven's son, so Mrs Medlock had to listen to what he said.

'Don't tell my father about this,' said Colin. 'He would stop Mary from coming and Mary makes me very happy.'

Mrs Medlock nodded. She put down the tray of soup and left.

After that day, Mary would work in the secret garden every morning. Then, she would go to see Colin.

Mary thought Colin was easy to talk to. Even when they argued, they were soon laughing again.

Mary thought this must be what it was like to have a brother. She smiled.

Chapter 11

One day, in the secret garden, Dickon was trying to get the fountain to work.

Mary was sitting on the white swing. Dickon had **oiled** it so it didn't creak anymore. Soon, Mary fell asleep.

She woke up to Dickon gently shaking her awake. She had been asleep for over an hour!

oiled - *To put oil on rusty or stiff metal. Oil helps the metal to move and bend at its joints.*

Mary ran out of the garden and into Colin's room.

'Where have you been?' asked Colin, angrily.

'I … fell … asleep!' said Mary, out of breath.

Colin started to **lose his temper**, but Mary quickly sat down on Colin's bed and started to **explain**.

lose his temper - When someone starts to get very angry.

explain - To help someone understand something.

Mary told Colin all about the secret garden and how Dickon was helping her.

Colin looked like he was about to cry. The secret garden made him think of his mum, who had died.

'I ... I think I should go to the garden,' he said.

Chapter 12

Surprisingly, Mrs Medlock helped Mary to get Colin into the garden.

She pushed Colin on his **wicker** *and wooden wheelchair to the garden.*

Mary walked next to them.

wicker - *Twigs that can be made into things like baskets and chairs.*

Dickon was waiting for them at the secret garden. Mrs Medlock left them when they went inside.

'It's magical!' said Colin.

He loved looking at the plants and the fountain that Dickon had fixed earlier. The only thing Colin wanted to change was to add some fish into the fountain.

The children played in the garden. Mary and Dickon showed Colin all of their favourite places.

Suddenly, Ben Weatherstaff looked over the garden wall.

'You shouldn't be in there!
It's locked up. Master Colin, you're too weak to be outdoors!' said Ben.

Colin was annoyed that everyone always told him what he could and couldn't do.

He held tightly on to the wheelchair for support. With his feet on the ground and his arms shaking, he began to lift himself out of his seat until he was standing.

Chapter 13

As the weeks passed, Colin spent more time in the garden with Mary, Dickon and Martha. He grew stronger every day.

Soon, Colin didn't need his wheelchair. He walked all the way to the garden by himself.

But when his father, Mr Craven, came back, Colin thought he wouldn't be allowed in the garden.

'You should show your father you are better now,' said Mary.

'I can't,' said Colin, sadly. 'This garden would remind my father of my mother. It would make him too sad.'

Dickon wanted to help Colin feel happy again, so he started a game of tag.

The children began to laugh again as Colin chased them all around the garden.

But soon, everyone except Colin became silent.

Standing behind Colin was his father, Mr Craven.

'My dearest boy!' said Mr Craven. 'You're playing and running!'

Mr Craven told the children that Mrs Medlock had explained everything to him and he came to the garden to find them.

At first, he was angry. But now he was just happy that Colin felt better.

As Colin hugged his father,
Mary felt sad.

Now that Colin was better, she was worried that he wouldn't need her anymore.

She tried to walk away, but Mr Craven stopped her.

'Mary, without you, none of this would have happened. This garden belongs to our family, and now we are your family,' said Mr Craven.

Mary smiled as Mr Craven hugged her.

She had found a family at last! A family and a garden of her own.

The End.

Frances Hodgson Burnett

Frances Hodgson Burnett was born in England in 1849. When she was 16 years old, she moved to the United States with her family.

At 19 years old, Burnett's story *The Secret Garden* was published in *The American Magazine* before being published as a book in 1911. It is still one of Burnett's most famous books.